Zip and

Episode Two:
The Spaceship

by Stan Cullimore

This is Blast. You may think that he is a post-box.
But he is not! He is a shape-changing alien.

This is Zip. You may think that she is a lamppost. But she is not! She is a shape-changing alien, too.

Zip and Blast come from a purple planet far away. They want to go back home but they can't find their spaceship.

"I'm hungry," said Zip.

"So am I," said Blast. "But we don't have time to look for food. We have to find our spaceship."

Blast stopped and looked in a shop window. He had an idea.

" Zip, I'm going to change into one of those things," said Blast.

"What is it?" asked Zip.
"It's a telescope. It helps you see things that are a long way off."

Blast changed shape. He changed into a big telescope.
"Take a look, Zip."
Zip put her eye to one end of the Blast telescope.
She looked all around.
"Can you see anything?" asked Blast.

"Yes, I can see something flying across the sky,"
said Zip.
"Is it our spaceship?" asked Blast.

"No, it's a plane," replied Zip.
"Can you see anything else?" asked Blast.

"Yes," said Zip. "I can see a dog."
"This is no good," said Blast. "I am going to change back into a post-box."

Blast changed back into a post-box. He looked around. "Where are you, Zip?"

Then he saw her. Zip had changed into a racing car. She was racing down the road.

Blast changed into a motorbike. He shot after Zip.
"Have you seen our spaceship?" he shouted.
"Yes," shouted Zip. She stopped by the side of the
road. So did Blast.

Zip changed into a very big hammer.

"What are you doing?" asked Blast.
"I told you, I'm hungry," replied Zip. "I want some chocolate!"

Blast changed back into a post-box. He ran over to the chocolate machine.

"Stop! You can't hit this machine," he said.

"Why not?" asked Zip.

"You will break it."

Zip changed back into a lamppost. She started
banging all the buttons on the chocolate machine.
The machine went BLEEP, BLEEP, BANG. It spat out
two bars of chocolate. Then it went dead.
"You've broken it!" said Blast.
"That's sad," said Zip. "Have some chocolate …"

"You said that you saw our spaceship," said Blast. "Where is it?"

"It's up there," replied Zip. "It's on top of that office block."

"Well done, Zip!" said Blast. "Now all we have to do is get up there."

"That's easy," said Zip.

She changed into a spider robot. She began to climb up the office block.

Zip went up and up. "Look at me, Blast," she shouted. "Am I a clever alien – or what?"

"Watch what you're doing," Blast shouted. But Zip did not hear him.

Zip put some of her spider legs on a window.
They slipped and Zip fell. She fell down and down.
She landed on Blast.
"How did you know I was going to fall?" asked Zip.
"You always do," said Blast.

Zip changed back into a lamppost. Blast changed
back into a post-box.

"I have to think," said Blast. "How can we get up
there to our spaceship?"
"I've got a really good idea," said Zip.

She changed into a small rocket.

"Get on my back," she said. "I will shoot up into the sky and then land by our spaceship."
Blast looked at Zip. He shook his head. "No, I've got a better idea."

Zip changed back into a lamppost. "OK. So what do we do?"

Blast smiled. "We go inside and use the lift."

Zip and Blast got into the lift. They went all the way up to the top of the office block.

When they got to the top of the office block they saw the spaceship.

"I'll just open the door," said Zip.

"NO!" cried Blast. "Don't you press any buttons – I'll do it."

Zip pressed the green button. The door slid open.

The two shape-changing aliens looked at each other.
They both smiled. Then they went inside their
spaceship. The door closed behind them.
They both sat down.

"It's nice to be back inside the spaceship, isn't it, Blast?" said Zip.

"Don't talk to me, Zip," replied Blast. He looked at all the buttons in front of him. There were a lot of them. "I have got to work out which button to press," he said.

"I will find us something to eat," said Zip. "I am so hungry!" She looked around. "Now where is the button to open the food tray?"

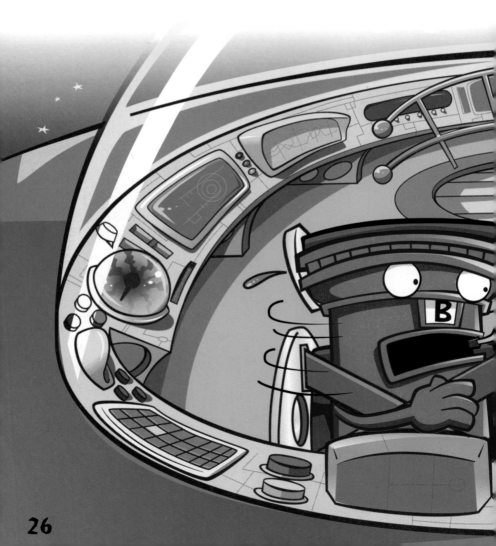

She saw a big blue button on the side. "There it is," said Zip.
"NO, DON'T PRESS THAT ONE!" cried Blast.
But it was too late. Zip had already pressed the button.

Blast put his head in his hands. "Oh dear. We're in trouble now. Big trouble."

"Why?" asked Zip.

"Because you pressed the big, blue button," said Blast sadly.

"Which button was I supposed to press?" asked Zip.

"None of them," replied Blast. "Pressing buttons is my job."

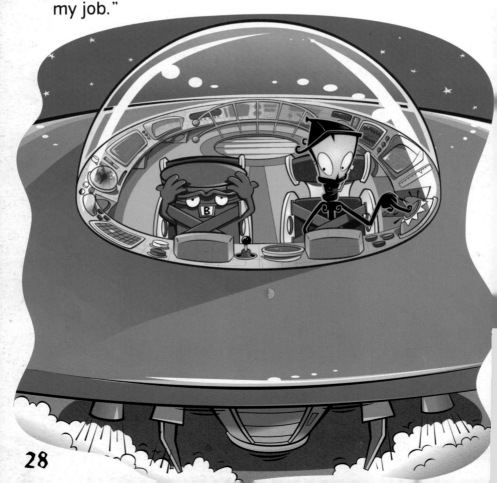

The spaceship began to shake. It went up into the air.
It shot across the sky. It stopped.
"That wasn't so bad, was it?" said Zip.
Suddenly the spaceship fell out of the sky. It fell like a
stone. It did not stop falling until it hit the ground.

The spaceship broke into a hundred little bits.
"I think the spaceship is broken," said Zip.
"I think you are right," said Blast. He looked at Zip.

"Zip," said Blast slowly. "I have got a really good idea."

"What is it, Blast?" asked Zip.

"DON'T EVER PRESS A BUTTON AGAIN!"
shouted Blast.